First published in Great Britain in 1993
by Simon & Schuster Young Books
Campus 400
Maylands Avenue
Hemel Hempstead
Herts HP2 7EZ

Typeset in 15/23pt Meridien by Goodfellow & Egan Ltd, Cambridge
Printed and bound in Portugal by Ediçoes ASA

British Library Cataloguing in Publication Data available

ISBN 0 7500 1381 8
ISBN 0 7500 1382 6 (pbk)

Roy Apps

A VAMPIRE IN THE FAMILY

Illustrated by Doffy Weir

SIMON & SCHUSTER
YOUNG BOOKS

Chapter One

The crisp winter morning sunlight streamed through Bruce's bedroom window. It fell right across his face, which was fair and freckled like a spicy sausage.

But Bruce slept on.

"Bruce! Get yourself up, you great lazy, lolloping layabout!" yelled his mum from the bottom of the stairs.

But Bruce slept on.

The alarm clock rattled and rang until the whole house shook like a strawberry jelly.

But Bruce slept on.

Then, from the next room, came a hideous roar.

"YER-ROWWW!"

Bruce leapt out of bed with a start.

You might have thought that there was a *tyrannosaurus rex* in there and that it had sat down on a drawing pin. But you would have been wrong.

It was Bruce's grandad.

"Bruce! The curtains!" growled Grandad's
gruff voice from beneath the bedclothes, as
Bruce poked his head round the bedroom door.

You might think Bruce's grandad wanted his
curtains thrown open to let in the sunlight, but
you'd be wrong. *He wanted them pulled tight, so
that his room was as dark as a cellar.*

8

"That's better," said Bruce's grandad. "Now I can watch the box."

You might think the box that Grandad was going to watch was a TV, but you'd be wrong. *It was a coffin.*

The reason Bruce's grandad spent all day in the dark staring at a coffin was simple.

But sinister.

. . . Bruce's grandad was a VAMPIRE.

Now it might seem that having a vampire in the family would be pretty exciting, but Bruce didn't think so. Because everybody's mum and dad said, "Now don't go playing with that Bruce. There's a vampire in his family."

So when the bell rang for end of school and everyone rushed out home in small huddles and in big gangs, Bruce always found himself on his own.

Until one day, when a new girl arrived at school. And because she was new she found herself on her own too.

"Hey! Chuck, wait for me!" she yelled to an astonished Bruce.

"My name's not Chuck, it's Bruce," said Bruce.

"That seems to me a very good reason why I should carry on calling you Chuck," said the new girl. "My name is Miranda Arkwright. We've moved into the chip shop on the corner.

Back in Lancashire I used to be leader of the
'Headless Mummies' gang. I chew up black
beetles with my bare teeth. What gang are you
in?"

"I'm not in any gang," sighed Bruce.

"Why not?" asked the former leader of the
'Headless Mummies'.

"Because . . ." But Bruce didn't want to tell
his new friend about there being a vampire in
his family.

"Tell you what, Chuck," said Miranda, when they reached Bruce's house, "I'll come round to your house after school tomorrow and we'll start a gang of our own."

Bruce shook his head sadly. "No one's allowed in our house. You see, it's my grandad . . ."

He looked up at the curtains drawn tightly
across his grandad's bedroom window.

"Is he poorly?" asked Miranda.

Bruce nodded. "Very. He's just skin and
bone. And ever so pale."

"Sounds like his blood," said Miranda.

14

"Not so much *his* blood, as other people's," muttered Bruce darkly.

"Tell you what, Chuck," said Miranda. "Why don't you come round to our place instead. It's as good a place as any to start a gang." And she turned on her heel and dashed off in the direction of the chip shop on the corner.

Bruce sighed. He'd made up his mind. Something would *definitely* have to be done about the vampire in his family.

"Grandad," said Bruce, in his most determined voice, "I've definitely decided. Vampiring isn't a decent sort of hobby for a man of your age. You've got to give it up."

Bruce was sitting on the coffin in the semi-darkness in his grandad's room, working his way through the plate of salad cream sandwiches that his mum had left out for his tea.

"I'll *fang* you not to tell me what I can and can't do, my boy," snapped Bruce's grandad. "I'm old enough to be your grandfather, you know."

"Grandad, you *are* my grandfather," sighed Bruce.

"Eh? Do what? Oh yes. So I am."

Bruce's grandad was busily chomping his way through a large bag of extra chewy toffees. He did this every day, to exercise his jaws.

"Why don't you take up the kind of hobby that normal grandads have, like growing onions?"

"And where's the grisly gruesomeness in growing onions, may I ask?" Bruce's grandad replied firmly. "Anyway, drawing blood from the dimply necks of young maidens has become something of a habit."

"I learnt to stop biting my finger nails," said Bruce. "I don't see why you can't learn to stop biting necks."

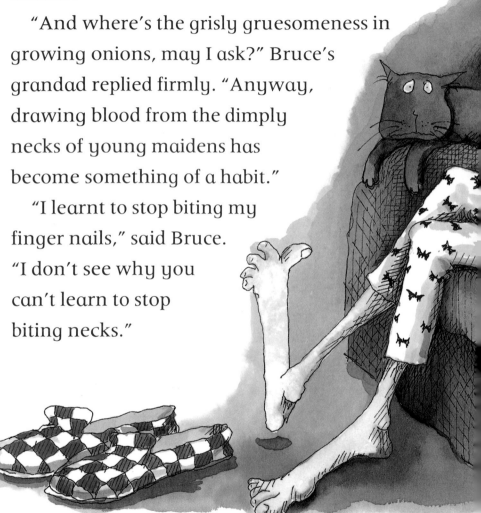

"Never, never, never!" insisted Grandad.

The winter's afternoon was growing quickly darker. Already, Grandad's fangs seemed to be growing longer and longer and Bruce could see them glinting in the gathering gloom. He sighed. He could see no way in which he would be able to conceal the awful truth about the vampire in his family from Miranda. And once she found out, she certainly wouldn't want him in her gang.

Grandad took another big bite from a huge
chewy toffee.

"YE-OWWW!" he suddenly yelled. He
clutched his jaw and leapt into the air so high
the top of his head scraped the ceiling.

"What's the matter, Grandad?" asked Bruce.

"It's my fangs! Don't just stand there boy, get
me to a dentist!"

Chapter Three

"I'm not going out dressed up like a blessed lollipop!" growled Grandad, as Bruce tried to wrap a red-and-pink striped scarf round his face.

"It'll stop you frightening people with your fangs."

"I won't *bite*," said Grandad, "not with the toothache I've got."

As they passed the chip shop on the corner, Bruce spotted Miranda behind the counter, taking orders. He hurried by, afraid she might see him with his Grandad and start asking awkward questions.

They turned into a long, tree-lined street full of big houses. They knocked on a big red door, on which was a gold plaque that read: *Mr Black: Dental Surgeon.*

"Now, which teeth are giving you problems?" The dental nurse smiled kindly at Grandad over a pair of large black-rimmed glasses.

"These two," said Grandad, and before Bruce could stop him, he'd unwrapped his scarf and was bending low over the dental nurse's dimply neck.

"No, Grandad!" shouted Bruce.

"Eeeeik!" yelled the dental nurse and fell down in a dead faint.

"Run for it, Grandad!" yelled Bruce.

The gold plaque on the door of the house next door read: *Ms Decker: Dental Surgeon.*

As they entered the surgery, Bruce could see his grandad fixing his eyes on Ms Decker's neck.

"Don't you dare, Grandad!" hissed Bruce.

"Sit down in the chair, please, and remove your scarf," said Ms Decker, and she turned towards her trolley of shiny silver instruments.

Bruce's grandad unwrapped his scarf and
bent low over Ms Decker's long smooth neck.

"No, Grandad!"
yelled Bruce. But
already Ms Decker
had wheeled round
and stuffed a wad of
cotton wool as big as a
prize fighter's fist into
Grandad's mouth.

I see your grandfather's a vampire," said Ms Decker.

"GRRRR!" growled Grandad through a mouthful of cotton wool.

Bruce sighed and nodded.

"These fangs of his are in a dreadful state."

"Is it because he spends all night going about biting people's necks?" asked Bruce accusingly.

"No." Ms Decker shook her head. "It's because he spends all day biting chewy toffees." And in a flash she'd tugged out Grandad's fangs and popped them into a glass saucer.

Then she took the cotton wool from his mouth. His gums drooped sadly over his bottom jaw. He had a face like a goldfish.

"Don't worry," Ms Decker said. "I'm sure I've got a nice new set of false teeth somewhere that will fit."

Grandad's new teeth were as shiny and as straight as a rock star's.

"These teeth aren't any blessed good for a vampire!" shouted Grandad. "All I need is a couple of sticks and I could hire myself out as a one-man xylophone!"

Ms Decker shrugged. "I'm sorry," she said. "But *fangs aren't what they used to be.*"

Chapter Four

That night, Bruce's
grandad went out
vampiring, but came
back again after
half an hour.

"Trying to get a decent bite of a neck with
these teeth," he groaned, "is like trying to eat a
bag of chips with a pair of mittens on!" and he
stomped off upstairs.

Bruce and his mum sat down to watch the
telly in peace.

Suddenly: "GR-RRRR!" came the sound from Grandad's room. "GR-RRRR!"

Bruce bounded up the stairs and poked his head round the door. His grandad was sitting on his bed. In his hand were his new teeth and stuck between the teeth was a huge chewy toffee.

"Every time I bite into a toffee, it pulls these blesshed teeth out!" moaned Grandad.

Next morning, Bruce was woken by a
banging and a clattering coming from his
grandad's bedroom.

Bruce went in. The curtains were drawn and
sunlight was pouring in through the open
window. Grandad was chopping up his coffin
with a mighty axe.

"I can't go on," he growled at Bruce. "My vampiring days are over."

"*Fang* goodness for that," said Bruce, whooping for joy. "Now nobody will be able to accuse us of having a vampire in our family. Now you can get a proper hobby like growing onions, just like a normal grandad."

Chapter Five

"Hey, Chuck! Don't forget we're meeting at my house to start a gang!" Miranda called after him on the way out of school.

Bruce knew he should have felt really happy, now that there wasn't a vampire in his family any more, but all day long he had felt uneasy about his grandad.

"I've just got to pop
home for something,"
he said to Miranda.
"I won't be a minute.
See you at your place."

Grandad was sitting on his bed, as still as a
statue, with his head in his hands.

"What is it, Grandad?"
Grandad sighed.
"Now that I'm not a
vampire any more, I've
got nothing left," he
said. "Vampiring was
my life."

"I'm sure you'll enjoy growing onions like a normal grandad."

Grandad sighed and shook his head.

"When my vampire friends saw my new teeth last night they all laughed at me. One of them said he'd be surprised if I could suck the jam out of a jammie dodger. Someone else stuck an apple in my mouth and said I might not be a vampire any more, but I did make a very good *fruit gum*!"

Grandad looked so sad, Bruce almost wished he could get his old fangs back for him. He said, "I'm going round Miranda's for tea. Why don't you come, Grandad? It'll cheer you up. I'm sure her mum won't mind."

"Hellow, Chuck!" said Miranda's mum when Bruce and Grandad walked into the chip shop on the corner. She turned to Grandad. "I expect you'd fancy a bite, wouldn't you?"

Grandad looked at Miranda's mum's pink, fleshy neck, bared his new false teeth for just a moment, then shook his head sadly.

"Of course he would," said Bruce quickly. "She means a *bite* of fish and chips, not a *bite* of neck!" he hissed in his grandad's ear.

"You and your grandad go on upstairs to the flat. Miranda's already up there."

"This is my grandad," said Bruce.

"Hello," said Miranda, and remembering that Bruce had told her his grandad was poorly, she asked politely, "and how's your blood?"

"My blood? It's a bit old for drinking, I'm afraid, my dear. You'd be better off trying a younger vintage."

"Er . . . just one of his little jokes . . ." stammered Bruce quickly.

38

The door opened and
in came a man about
Grandad's age.

"This is my Great-Uncle Arnold," said
Miranda. "He's having tea with us."

Bruce, Miranda, Grandad and Great-Uncle
Arnold sat down to a fish and chip tea.
Grandad still looked very unhappy and Bruce
still felt uneasy.

"Would you mind passing me the congealed blood?" Grandad asked Miranda, pointing to a big red bottle.

"That's tomato ketchup!" hissed Bruce, wriggling uncomfortably in his chair.

Miranda shot Bruce a very funny look, and Great-Uncle Arnold shot Grandad an even funnier one. Bruce wished he had left Grandad at home. Miranda would never want him in her gang now.

"Bruce and I have got to decide on a name
for our gang," announced Miranda,
importantly.

Great-Uncle Arnold beckoned silently to
Grandad and the two old gentlemen went
through to the sitting and shut the door.

Bruce sighed. "Look,
Miranda," he said. "You
might as well know. The
reason I'm not in anyone's
gang is that my grandad
is — or rather was . . ."
he paused, then whispered,
". . . a vampire!"

Miranda chuckled, "Oh, I guessed that, Chuck!"

"You did?" asked a startled Bruce.

"Of course," laughed Miranda.

"And you don't mind?"

"No you see, my uncle is a—"

But before she could finish, there came a deafening, chilling howl from the direction of the sitting room. Bruce shivered in his seat. Miranda ran to the sitting room door and flung it open.

Bruce gasped.

From the depths of a large, comfortable armchair there rose – a WEREWOLF!

"As I was saying, Chuck, my uncle's a werewolf."

Bruce gulped. But not just at Miranda's werewolf uncle. For out of the other armchair there rose another werewolf, whose pearly white teeth were all too familiar to Bruce.

"Grandad!"

"You were right, Bruce," howled Grandad
from behind his thick, brown wolf-like
whiskers. "Vampiring is no sort of hobby for an
old-fangled man of my age. I've decided to join
Arnold's werewolf pack, instead!"

"What are you going to call your gang then?" growled Great-Uncle Arnold.

"I don't know," said Miranda.

"You need the sort of name you can *get your teeth into*!" howled Bruce's grandad.

"Something *snappy*," growled Uncle Arnold.

"What about the *Fang* Gang?" declared Miranda. "What do you think, Bruce?"

Bruce grinned. "There's only one word for it," he said. "*Fang*tastic!"

Look out for more hilarious creepy books in the Storybooks series:

The Twitches by Roy Apps
Illustrated by Carla Daly

Gert and Lil have made a grand decision: they are going to give up witching and make a brand new start. But things for these accident-prone twin witches don't exactly go as planned . . .

The Twitches on Horriday by Roy Apps
Illustrated by Carla Daly

Gert and Lil are delighted when they win a fancy dress competition – and the prize is a free trip to Spain. After creating havoc in the smart hotel, the manager banishes them to the old goatshed, which is just the kind of luxury they appreciate!

Wonderwitch by Helen Muir
Illustrated by Linda Birch

Wonderwitch has everything a witch needs – a tall hat, a black cat and a broomstick. But she's getting a bit bored with her old spells, and decides to try something quite different!

Wonderwitch and the Rooftop Cats by Helen Muir
Illustrated by Linda Birch

Seeing the homeless cats on the roof, Wonderwitch hits on a brilliant new business idea. But, as usual when Wonderwitch tries one of her plans, things go horribly wrong.

The Magic of the Mummy by Terry Deary
Illustrated by Katey Farrell

When Cleo, Beryl and Edward visit the Museum of Mystery to try and decifer the mummy's secret message, Cleo accidentally says the spell which brings the mummy to life. Things are looking black, until Cleo manages to thwart the mummy's evil plan to take over the world . . .